SO-AEK-898

JE   .   Brown, Marc Tolon.
BRO   Arthur and the new
READER   kid

STEP INTO READING®

STEP **3**

MARC BROWN

ARTHUR and the NEW KID

AMHERST PUBLIC LIBRARY
221 SPRING STREET
AMHERST, OHIO 44001

A Sticker Book

Random House New York

Copyright © 2004 by Marc Brown. All rights reserved under International and Pan-American Copyright Conventions. Published in the United States by Random House Children's Books, a division of Random House, Inc., New York, and simultaneously in Canada by Random House of Canada Limited, Toronto.

www.stepintoreading.com

Educators and librarians, for a variety of teaching tools, visit us at www.randomhouse.com/teachers

Library of Congress Cataloging-in-Publication Data
Brown, Marc Tolon.
Arthur and the new kid / Marc Brown. — 1st ed.
p.   cm. — (Step into reading. A step 3 sticker book.)
SUMMARY: Arthur and his friends discover that the new boy at school is different from what they first thought.
ISBN 0-375-81381-0 (trade) — ISBN 0-375-91381-5 (lib. bdg.)
[1. Schools—Fiction. 2. Interpersonal relations—Fiction. 3. Aardvark—Fiction. 4. Cats—Fiction. 5. Animals—Fiction.]
I. Title. II. Series: Step into reading sticker books. Step 3.
PZ7.B81618Agt 2004 [E]—dc21 2003002664

Printed in the United States of America First Edition 10 9 8 7 6 5 4 3 2 1

STEP INTO READING, RANDOM HOUSE, and the Random House colophon are registered trademarks of Random House, Inc.
ARTHUR is a registered trademark of Marc Brown.

writing assignment
Your
Summer
Vacation

Arthur's class was writing
about their summer vacation.
Suddenly the door opened.
In walked someone new.
"This is Norbert," said Mr. Ratburn.
"He has just moved to Elwood City.
Take a seat anywhere, Norbert."

Norbert took a seat
in the back near no one.
"He thinks he's too good for us,"
whispered Francine.
"Yeah," said Buster.
"Look at his jacket."

Soon it was lunchtime.
Arthur and his friends
sat together.
"Look," said Muffy.
"Here comes Norbert the Nerd."

Norbert walked right past them.
"He's sitting with fourth graders!"
said the Brain.
"He's stuck up," said Francine.
"Maybe he's just shy," said Arthur.

"I bet he's rich," said Francine.
"He doesn't bring his lunch.
He buys two slices of pizza,
a milk shake, and lemon cake."
"Yeah," said Buster.
"He's too cool for this school."

After lunch Mr. Ratburn said,
"Norbert, why don't you
sit near the others."
Norbert moved up next to Francine.
"Don't worry," she said.
"I take a bath every night."
Everyone laughed.

"Here's a problem," said Mr. Ratburn.
"If a rooster laid two eggs
in a bird nest,
five eggs in the pig pen,
and three eggs in the barn,
how many eggs did
the farmer find?"

The class was quiet.

"Put on your thinking caps,"

said Mr. Ratburn.

But no one said a word.

"No answer, no recess,"

said Mr. Ratburn.

Then Norbert whispered something

to Francine.

Francine raised her hand.

"Yes, Francine," said Mr. Ratburn.

"The farmer didn't find any eggs," she said. "Roosters don't lay eggs!"

Mr. Ratburn smiled.

"Thank you, Francine," he said.

"Or should I thank Norbert?"

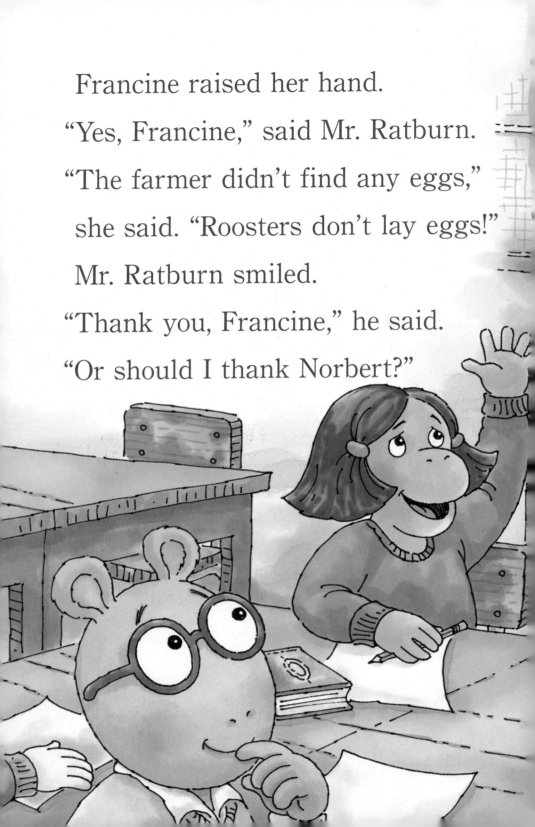

At recess Arthur and his friends
played soccer.
Norbert watched Buster kick
the ball off the field.
Norbert jumped up.
He bounced the ball
off his head and back to Buster.
"Wow!" said Francine.
"He's really good."

"Want to play?"
Arthur asked Norbert.
"Sure," he answered.
And he kicked in two goals
before recess ended.

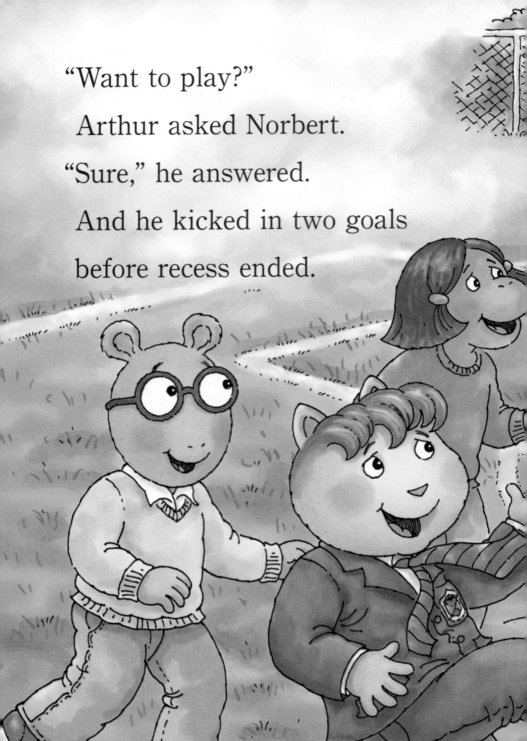

Francine ran up to Norbert.
"Thanks for getting us recess.
You're really smart!" she said.
Norbert blushed.
"Oh, that rooster question
is in a riddle book I have,"
he said.

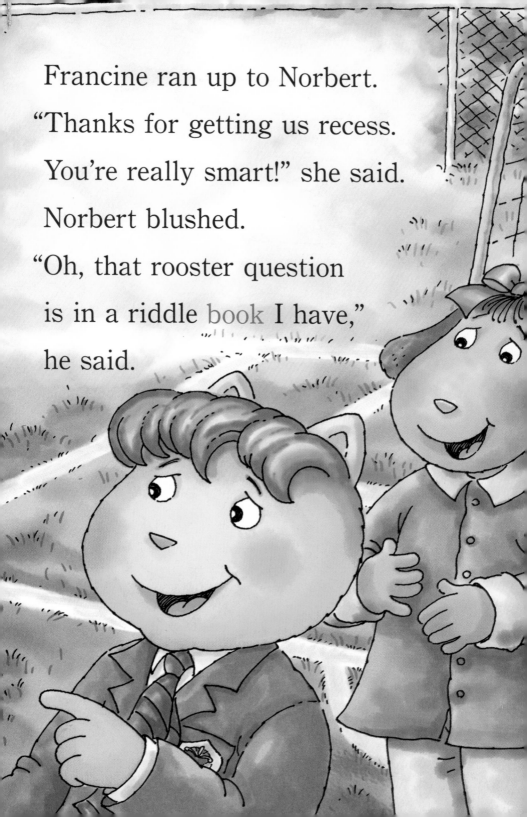

After school Arthur and Buster
asked Norbert to go
to Arthur's house.
"Okay," said Norbert,
and he pulled off his tie.
"I had to wear this tie
and jacket at my last school.
My mother made me wear it today.
But I won't wear it again!"
he said.

"Way to go, Norbert!"
said Arthur and Buster.
"Call me Bert," said Norbert.
"High five!" said Arthur.
And they did.

FEB   2006

JE   Brown, Marc Tolon.
BRO   Arthur and the new
READER   kid

AMHERST PUBLIC LIBRARY
221 SPRING STREET
AMHERST, OHIO 44001

DISCARD